ISBN: 9780578730493 (Paperback)

Library of Congress Control Number: 2020941389

Any references to historical events, real people, or real places are used fictitiously. Names, characters, and places are products of the author's imagination.

Visit
Abeni Publishing
everythingabeni.com

01

The Best Day Ever!

The story of how my hair fell out begins the day after the best day ever! My Aunt Patty and Uncle Robby got married, and my sister, Suzie, and I were in the wedding. We were junior bridesmaids, because Aunt Patty claimed we were too old to be flower girls. I was 11 and Suzie was almost 9. The morning of the wedding, Suzie and I went to the hair salon with Mom and Aunt Patty and had our hair styled in fancy braids all over our head and then curled at the bottom. We even had our nails painted light pink, and we got to wear a little mascara and lip gloss. I sported a long pale pink dress and sparkly shoes with what Mom calls "kitten heels." Suzie had to wear flats, but her dress was exactly the same as mine. Mom wore a pale pink short dress with matching heels.

Mom, Suzie, Grampy, Aunt Patty, and I gathered in the vestibule of the church, which was filled with Aunt Patty and Uncle Robby's closest friends and family. When the music started, Mom hugged Aunt Patty tightly and blew kisses to Suzie and me. Mom opened the door to the church and, holding her bouquet of white roses in front of her, slowly walked down the aisle. Suzie and I each held our bouquets in front of us, like Mom did, and followed her down the aisle. Suzie was trying to go too fast, but soon matched her steps with mine, and we smiled our way down the aisle in perfect sync. We took our places on either side of Mom and turned around just as the music changed. Everyone in the church stood to watch Aunt Patty float down the aisle like a princess. She wore a white strapless dress with a big puffy skirt. Her tiara sparkled as she leaned in to kiss Grampy on the cheek before turning to Uncle Robby, who looked like he might cry.

"You're stunning!" he whispered to Aunt Patty as he took her hand, and they walked up onto the altar.

At the reception, we sat at the head table with Mom, Dad, Aunt Patty, and Uncle Robby. A few people, including Mom, stood up and recalled nice things and fun memories about Aunt Patty and Uncle Robby, then we all clinked glasses and drank sparkling cider. After dinner, we danced all night, stopping only to watch Aunt Patty and Uncle Robby cut the cake. Suzie and I were the only kids there, so we got to stay up way past 10.

"Let's just take your braids out in the morning," Mom insisted in the car on the way home. Suzie had already fallen asleep, and I just smiled and nodded, thinking about the day. It was one of those days when you're kind of sad when it's over, because it was

THAT good and you can't imagine anything ever being quite that amazing again.

The next morning I woke up late to the smell of pancakes and sausages. Dad was making his Sunday "Daddy breakfast."
"Suzie!" I called from my bed, "Good morning! Wasn't that the best day ever?"
"So fun," she recalled, and we both headed downstairs to eat.
"Good morning, Francie!" Mom greeted. "Good morning, Suz! Did you have fun yesterday?"
"I can't wait for my own wedding someday! I want to be a bride like Aunt Patty!" I exclaimed.
"Me too!" Suzie agreed.
Dad laughed. "Well, let's not rush into anything," he cautioned, as he flipped pancakes onto plates.
"Sausages and syrup are on the table, girls," he said. "Let me get you some milk."
I drenched my pancakes in syrup and handed the bottle to Suzie.
"Two milks for the two beautiful flower girls!" Dad proclaimed.
"Junior Bridesmaids!" Mom, Suzie, and I cheered in unison, reminding him for probably the twelfth time.
"Well, either way, you two were as pretty as the bride, and your hair still looks beautiful this morning."
"You probably shouldn't say that in front of my sister," Mom teased Dad.
After pancakes, we had to get ready for church.
"Let's just take the braids out after church, girls," Mom suggested. "We don't have a lot of time. Go on and get dressed."

We made it to church just in time for the greeter, Mr. Smith, to give Suzie and me his regular greeting. "Good morning lovely ladies!"

This week he added something special. "What beautiful hair you both have this morning."

"They were in a wedding," Dad informed him. "Uh ... junior bridesmaids!"

"Very nice," Mr. Smith replied, as Mom hurried us to our pew.

After church, we all sat down in the living room, and Mom started to take out Suzie's braids. Dad sat me on his lap and started to take out mine.

"Gosh, there's a lot of hair coming out with your braids, Bug," Dad noticed. "Elaine, is Suzie losing a lot of hair, too? Maybe these braids weren't the best idea?"

"Uh, Suzie's hair is fine, Ed," Mom verified. "Let me see."

As Mom got up and walked over to look at my head, Dad lifted his hands to show her the hair he was holding. His hands were full, and he hadn't even finished taking out my braids.

02
The Diagnosis

A few weeks later, Mom said we were going to see a dermatologist named Dr. Miller. My hair was still falling out, and it was getting more and more difficult to hide. Mom was getting creative with my hairstyles, parting my hair on the other side, but even that wasn't working anymore.

The drive to Dr. Miller's office took almost an hour. I wasn't sure why we couldn't just go to see Dr. Schaefer, our regular pediatrician, whose office was right near our house. Dr. Miller's office was in a hospital, and we had to walk down a long hall to get to it. Mom told the receptionist my name, and they called us back a few minutes later. Dr. Miller was a young female doctor with long brown hair tied back in a ponytail.

"Her hair is getting thinner and thinner," Mom started. "It's on her pillow and in the bathtub—" She started to cry before she could finish.

Dad took over. "We don't understand why Francie's hair is falling out. Her part is getting wider and wider. What can we do about this?"

"Francie, why don't you jump up on the table?" Dr. Miller asked. She looked at my head, moving my hair from side to side, the same way Mom had done when she was styling it. Then, without warning, Dr. Miller yanked a piece of my hair out.

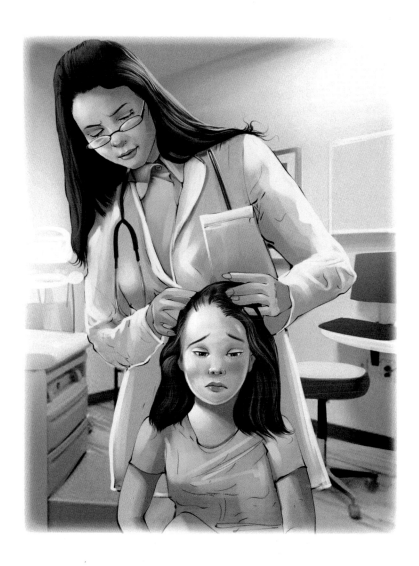

"Did that hurt?" she asked.

"No," I declared. "It didn't hurt at all." Dr. Miller frowned. Maybe I should have lied?

She took the hair with her and left the room. Mom, Dad, and I all sat quietly, and I watched the clock tick out six minutes until she finally returned.

"Well," Dr. Miller suggested, "I think you have what's called alopecia areata. It's an autoimmune disease, which means that your body thinks that your hair is an invader, so it purposely attacks it, causing it to fall out. The easiest way to explain it to your friends is to say that your body is allergic to your hair."

Dr. Miller turned to Mom and Dad, who both looked so nervous. "The problem with alopecia is that every case is different, so it's hard to know what will happen next. Francie's hair could grow back tomorrow or more could fall out. There's actually no way of knowing. I can give you some medicine to rub on her head at night. Sometimes, it helps to grow hair; sometimes it doesn't, but I think it's worth a try."

Mom and Dad both nodded nervously at the same time.

A nurse came into the room. She smiled at me and handed Mom some pamphlets with pictures of bald kids on the front. Mom quickly slipped them into her purse. Why would the nurse give us those? My hair was getting thinner. I wasn't going bald!

Mom and Dad took me to Shirley's, a diner around the corner from the hospital. I ordered grilled cheese and French fries, my favorite. Dad ordered a bowl of clam chowder and Mom ordered a chef's salad. Neither of them said anything while we waited for our food to come.

"Are you excited for basketball season?" Dad finally asked me after the waitress brought our food.

"I think we're going to be really good this year," I exclaimed, grateful for something different to talk about. My best friend Livy and I had been practicing all summer. She even went to a basketball camp at St. Joseph's College. She was already our best player, so we were going to be even better than last year.

"That's great!" Dad encouraged. He pushed his soup around. Mom hardly touched her salad. Neither of them seemed interested in hearing about basketball. Suddenly, I wasn't that excited about grilled cheese or French fries.

"What's going on?" I asked

Dad grabbed the bill. "Let's talk in the car."

Mom slid out of our booth, and I followed. She put her arm around me as we walked to the car.

When we got in, Mom and Dad didn't put their seatbelts on. Dad turned around in his seat so he was looking right at me. Mom turned around, too.

"No matter what happens with your hair, Francie," Dad began very slowly, "you know that Mom and I love you and think you're beautiful. If we seem sad, it's because we want everything in your life—and in Suzie's—to be perfect and easy for you. And even though we know that that isn't how life usually works, it makes us a little sad when something doesn't go perfectly for you. Like Dr. Miller said, we don't know what will happen next with your hair, but whatever it is, we'll get through it together." Then he winked at me and smiled, but it was a sad smile.

"And whatever happens, Daddy and I love you and think you're beautiful," Mom added, smiling just as sadly.

I couldn't help but wonder why they were overreacting. Dr. Miller said we didn't know what would happen next. She also said my hair might grow back tomorrow.

I guess they knew something I didn't, because over the next couple of weeks, my hair kept getting thinner and thinner. Mom would brush it before school every day, like she did when I was younger, only now she stroked it very slowly and gently. She combed it to the side and started to put it into a barrette, then brushed it to the other side, kind of like Dr. Miller had. Finally, she fastened the barrette into place.

"Look how pretty it looks to this side," she gushed, standing behind me in the mirror. "You look beautiful." Mom hadn't fussed this much over my hair in years.

When the barrettes stopped working, we tried cloth headbands, which helped disguise my growing forehead. My part wasn't just getting wider anymore; my hairline was receding, too, just like Grampy's.

Kids at school started staring at me and whispering behind their hands when I walked by. Livy assured me that it was all in my imagination. I wanted to believe her, but she was definitely in denial. Livy and I had been best friends since first grade when she moved here in the middle of the year. She was very tall, and sometimes, the boys in our class would talk about her, especially when she first moved here. However, she honestly didn't seem to notice that either.

03

To Cover Up or Not to Cover Up?

One day when I got home from school, Mom handed me a bag from the local store. The bag contained a pink sparkly bandana and a yellow baseball cap.

"Are these for me?"

"I talked to the school, and they gave you special permission to wear hats and bandanas to school starting tomorrow. What do you think? I picked up one of each for you," Mom explained with another sad smile.

"Thank you." I half-smiled back at her. Why would I want to wear hats or bandanas to school? They would only draw attention to me and cause more kids to stare and whisper. I just wanted my hair back. All of it!

"You don't have to wear them, Francie," Mom clarified. "I just wanted you to have them in case you decided you wanted them." She gave me a hug, and I ran up to my room, unsure of what I was going to do.

The next day, I decided to wear one of the hats to school. When I came downstairs for breakfast, Mom looked up from her coffee and started to say something, but just smiled her sad smile at me again. She wasn't sure what to say and, honestly, neither was I.

"Why not?" Suzie had said the night before when I asked her if she thought that I should start wearing them. "It can't hurt," she continued. "It's cool that you got special permission."

I chose the yellow baseball cap, because it was less noticeable, and it matched my yellow converse sneakers.

I told myself it was no big deal being the only kid wearing a hat to school, but as soon as I got to school, everyone started looking over their shoulders at me. Even Livy noticed the stares at lunch.

It was pretty much impossible not to notice. This one kid, Davey, was walking with his lunch tray and almost crashed into a wall because he was so entranced by my hat. Normally, I would've laughed, but there was nothing funny about people staring at me.

"No one cares about your hair," Livy tried her best to assure me, "Why don't you take off the hat?"

Livy wore her own difference (being tall) with confidence. Personally, I thought the boys were just jealous because they wished they were taller, especially when they played basketball in gym class and Livy blocked all of their shots.

"Not in my house!" the girls would shout when Livy blocked a shot from going into the basket. The boys didn't laugh.

Maybe Livy knew what she was talking about, I thought, as we threw away our trash after lunch. I took off the yellow hat and stuffed it in my backpack, just as the bell rang and we headed to math class together.

Suddenly, it felt like I was a clown or a juggler walking through school. Everywhere I turned, someone was looking at me. Livy stuck to me like glue, but, grateful as I was to have her beside me, it was hard to pay attention in class or even to walk through the halls with my head up. I just wanted to be home where I was safe from the stares and whispers. When the last bell of the day finally rang, I gathered my things and hurried to the walker line.

"Bye!" Livy shouted as we moved in opposite directions, and she went to catch her bus home. Then I saw Gertie, who I usually walked home with every day. We didn't hang out that much at school, but we lived in the same neighborhood. I ran to catch up with her, but she seemed to be walking extra fast today. Eventually, I gave up and started to walk alone.

At Main Street, Gertie had to stop for traffic, so I almost caught up with her. I changed my mind and slowed my pace, unsure what I could even talk about with her today. However, Gertie must have changed her mind, too. She stopped and waited, and I ended up walking beside her.

"I noticed you were wearing a hat this morning," Gertie mentioned.

"Yeah," I confirmed. "My mom thought I might be more comfortable wearing a hat to school these days, but then I was talking to Livy, and—"

Gertie interrupted me. "I think it's a good idea for you to wear a hat to school. You know, it would be easier for all of us. Don't take this the wrong way, but it's kind of hard for the rest of us to look at your head like that."

I'm not exactly sure what happened next or even if I responded. My face burned, and I just wanted to get away from Gertie. I bit my lip and walked in silence the rest of the way home, while she talked on and on about her upcoming trip to Cancun. I focused all of my energy on not crying in front of her until, finally, she turned left to head to her house, and I ran the rest of the way home.

04
FAKE IT 'TIL YOU MAKE IT

I stopped to compose myself when I got to my front door, hoping, as I turned the doorknob, that Mom wouldn't ask too many questions about my day. Suzie had Girl Scouts after school, so I knew all attention would be on me, which it usually was lately. Mom had baked some cookies and was pouring me a glass of milk when I walked into the kitchen.

"How was your day, honey?" Mom asked with the biggest smile she could muster.

"It was fine," I lied. "Everything was fine." I really didn't want to tell her about what Gertie said.

I couldn't even think about eating cookies at a time like this, so I told Mom I had a lot of homework and went up to my room. Mom sighed and didn't even pretend to smile, but revealing what Gertie said would only make her feel worse. I did my homework and tried to study, but I couldn't concentrate. I told Mom I wasn't hungry at dinner. I wasn't sure what to do, but I couldn't eat, and I couldn't study. I just lay on my bed and stared at the ceiling. Around 7:00, Dad knocked on my door. I quickly grabbed my history book and pretended I was studying. He came in with a dinner tray and set it on my desk.

"Meatloaf and mac and cheese! Your favorite!" he teased.

"Thanks, Dad," I responded.

"So, what happened at school today?" he asked. I looked at my dad. It was so hard to lie to him, but I just wasn't ready to tell him about Gertie.

"Nothing really happened, Dad," I dismissed, "I just feel like everyone is staring at me. I wish my hair would grow back."

"I know, Bug," Dad sighed "Mom and I do, too, but sometimes things happen that we have no control over. Just try to be brave, Francie. I like to say, 'Fake it till you make it.'"

"What do you mean?" I asked.

"Well, even if you aren't really feeling brave, just smile when people stare at you. Stand tall like you don't care what anyone thinks ... even if you do. Eventually, you won't care. You'll feel as brave as you're acting."

"Okay," I said. I wanted to believe him, but I wasn't convinced. "I'll try it."

"Awesome!" he replied. "And, most importantly, just remember that you're beautiful with or without hair, and Mom and I love you very much."

"I know," I confirmed, glancing in the mirror at my grandfatherly head. How could they possibly think I was beautiful?

"Why don't you finish your dinner and then come down for a game of Uno with Suzie and Mom?"

"Okay," I agreed. "I'll be down in a few minutes."

The next day, I sported the bandana to school. I knew the other kids were whispering and staring, but I took Dad's advice and pretended like I didn't notice or care. Sometimes, I felt like I was going to cry, but then Livy would be there, telling me a joke or a funny story about the boys in gym class. That definitely helped. After school, I walked home with Suzie. I hated the hats and bandanas, but I took Gertie's advice and wore them for the sake of everyone who had to look at my ugly bald head.

Besides Livy and some of my friends on our basketball team, the girls at school pretty much pretended I didn't exist. In some ways, I was grateful; all I really wanted was to be invisible and to blend in like everyone else. I didn't exactly want to be ignored, but it was easier dealing with that than with the boys at school. They seemed intent on making sure that I never forgot that I was different and going bald. This one boy, Jack, would whisper,

"Baldie," every time he saw me or walked past me. He'd pretend to sneeze and then say it into his hand. I did everything I could to ignore him, but my eyes would fill with tears, and I'm sure he saw that.

One day in math class, I knew Jack and another boy, Brandon, were sitting behind me when I felt something dripping onto my head. I looked up at the ceiling thinking that maybe there was a leak, and that's when I heard them laughing. Livy was sitting in front of me, so I tapped her on the shoulder.

"Is something in my hair?" I tried to whisper to her. I turned my head around so she could look, again hearing the boys in the back of the class laughing, but I didn't look in their direction. Livy pulled a spitball attached to a handful of hair from the wispies that stuck out of the bottom of my hat. We both gasped when she showed it to me, and Jack and Brandon burst out laughing uncontrollably.

"What's going on back there?" Mr. Hartman glared at the four of us.

Livy opened her mouth. I know she was about to tell him that the boys were throwing spit balls at me, but I quickly interjected, "Nothing. There was something in my hair, but I got it."

After class, Livy and I ran to the bathroom. She tried to remove the other eight spitballs from my hair, but I stopped her after two: because each time she pulled one out, another handful of hair would vanish with it.

"You should have let me tell Mr. Hartman," Livy grumbled. "Jack and Brandon should get detention for that."

"I know, but then it's just going to get worse," I told her. "Let's just try to ignore them." I knew it was easier said than done.

My home was my safe haven. My family didn't care about my hair or that I was going bald. So, as soon as I walked in the door, the hat came off. One day, Livy came home with me after school to hang out until basketball practice. I wasn't sure if I should keep my bandana on that day or take it off. Remembering Gertie's words, I decided to just leave it on, even though it was annoying to wear, and it kept sliding off.

As Livy and I played a game of checkers, I readjusted my bandana for the third time when Livy finally suggested, "Francie, why don't you just take it off?"

"Really?" I asked. "You don't mind?"

Abruptly, I blurted it out, "Gertie said it would be easier for everyone if I just wore a hat to school. I thought maybe you were just being nice."

"Me? Nice?" Livy joked. "I'm here to hang out with you. I don't care about your hair. And how does Gertie know what everyone thinks, anyway?"

I whipped off the bandana, and it landed in the kitchen, next to Mom's feet. I looked up as Mom picked it up and smiled. Even her eyes smiled this time.

05

28 HATS

One day I came home from school to find a big cardboard box sitting on the porch in front of the door. "FRANCIE" was written in big bold letters, and the box was decorated with hearts and flowers. Suzie and I were very excited to see what was inside, but we had to ask Mom for help to get the box through the door because it was so huge. Once inside, Mom used scissors to cut the top of the box open. Inside were dozens of hats, every kind I could imagine. There were ski caps in all different colors, baseball caps from a few different sports teams, a pretty plush hat that could be worn with a dress to church, and too many more to name.

"There's a card," Mom commented as Suzie and I pulled out hat after hat and tried them on. Mom handed me the card, and I read it out loud.

"Dear Francie,

We hope you like the hats. We picked them out just for you.

With love,

Your friends in Troop 646."

I looked at Mom, who was smiling through tears. When Dad came home, he got out his camera and took pictures of me in each of the twenty-eight hats. It was a fun night. It was nice to smile and laugh with Suzie and Mom and Dad. Yet, as I lay in bed that night, I wondered if the girls in Suzie's brownie troop preferred when I wore hats, like Gertie did?

06

WHO CAN I TRUST?

One evening, Mom and Dad said they were going out to dinner and that Hannah was going to babysit. Hannah was the best babysitter. Every time she came over she joked about how she knew us since we were born and had even changed our diapers. This was so embarrassing, but it made us all giggle, and Suzie and I secretly loved it. Hannah hadn't seen us in a long time, and I wondered if she knew I was going bald. When I heard her at the door, I quickly grabbed my hat and put it on. As I ran down to hug Hannah, Mom and Dad looked at each other, but I pretended not to notice and pulled Hannah into the kitchen to show her the homemade pizza kits that Mom had bought us for dinner.

We had a great time at home with Hannah while Mom and Dad went out to dinner. After we made pizzas and cleaned up, Hannah painted our nails and braided Suzie's hair.
"Do you want me to braid your hair, Francie?" She asked. I knew it was coming.

"Nah," I dismissed. "Not tonight." I wasn't even sure if I had enough hair left to braid, and even if I did, braiding it might make it fall out in Hannah's hands. That would be so embarrassing! Hannah just smiled and didn't ask questions. I thought about taking off my hat and revealing my bald head to Hannah, but I wasn't sure how she'd react, and I didn't want to make her feel uncomfortable. We had a lot of fun playing games and watching The Parent Trap, and the time slipped by swiftly.

"Guess it's time for bed," Hannah announced when the movie ended. It was way past ten, our weekend bedtime. We stretched and yawned and went upstairs to brush our teeth and get ready for bed. I climbed into my bed with my hat still on my head. I probably should have told Hannah about my alopecia when she first got to our house and Mom and Dad were still home, but now it felt like it was too late.

Hannah came in to kiss me good night. "Do you always wear a hat to bed, Francie?" She asked.

Before I knew what I was saying, I replied, "Yeah, my head gets cold." I immediately regretted the lie, but it was for Hannah's own good. She didn't need to see my balding head.

07

When Quitting Becomes Inevitable

On Tuesday night I had basketball practice.

"Maybe you don't need to wear a hat to practice, Francie," Dad suggested.

"I'll think about it," I told him, but now wasn't the time to stop wearing hats. I had started to lose one of my eyebrows, and most of my eyelashes had fallen out. A hat was no longer enough to cover up my alopecia, but it definitely disguised it.

Plus, everything was fine at basketball. No one said anything, and hanging out with Livy and my other friends usually made me forget all about being bald. I pulled on my little black beanie, which I always wore to practice. It reminded me of the hat Mom wore when she ran in the cold weather. It got a little sweaty on the inside, but it stayed on my head pretty well and didn't slide around during practice.

"See you all Saturday at St. Mary's for our first game," Coach Patterson reminded us at the end of practice. "Go Warriors!" We all put our hands in and repeated "Go Warriors!" before we ran outside to meet our parents.

St. Mary's was almost thirty minutes away, so we had to leave at noon on Saturday.

"Time to leave, girls," Mom yelled up the stairs, and Suzie and I ran down stairs. I grabbed a granola bar for the ride, my water bottle, and my beanie and jumped into the minivan, buckling in next to Suzie. As I got out of the car at St. Mary's, before we even entered the school, it seemed everyone was looking at me as if I were an alien or something. Were the people at home starting to get used to seeing me, or did I really look that much worse? Some of the older people, probably parents and grandparents, looked at me with very sad eyes. As I walked into the gym, an elderly woman approached me.

"Keep up the fight," she encouraged. "My daughter is in remission. Don't give up." I looked at Mom, and she started to explain to the woman that I didn't have cancer, but the woman kept walking. I don't think she heard Mom.

A little boy tugged on his dad's hand. "Look at that poor little girl." Suzie walked right up to them and said, "My sister has alopecia; her body is allergic to her hair." The dad apologized and looked really embarrassed.

Once inside, I found my team and, as I began warming up, the girls on the other team were not only whispering and staring, but they were also pointing at me and laughing. I heard one girl with red hair and freckles ask their coach, "Why is there a boy on their team?" Without even looking in my direction, he told her, "There are no boys on their team." I wished Suzie had been there to hear that one, but she was in the stands with Mom and Dad.

I took my place on the bench, hoping that the excitement of the game would make me invisible. Livy was playing great today. She was making every shot and blocking most of their shots. The gym erupted with applause when Livy made an amazing block. "Go Livy! Go Warriors!" chanted our parents as Livy took the ball down the court and made another basket. She was on fire today and looked so happy out there.

Watching Livy play basketball, it was easy to tell that when she was on that court, she forgot all about being tall or different. She was never one to brag, but she had to notice that, no matter who they played, she was so much better than everyone else out there, and her height was definitely an advantage. I guess it was like in art class when Mrs. Baldwin pointed out my work as an example to the other students in our class. It made me feel so proud that my heart felt like it might be too big for my chest sometimes. Maybe that's how Livy feels on the basketball court, I thought.

I was lost in these thoughts when Coach Patterson called, "Francie!" and signaled that she was putting me in the game. I high-fived Allison, who was coming out, and ran onto the court. The referee blew the whistle and gave the ball to Ellie. Ellie brought the ball up and passed it to Livy who passed it right to me. I was about to catch it when the girl with the red hair came out of nowhere and ran right into me. The next thing I knew, I was on the ground and so was my black beanie. There wasn't a sound in the gym, as I scrambled for my beanie, which had landed right next to Livy. I tried not to panic as Livy reached down and picked it up, glaring at the girl with red hair and then handing it to me. As I pulled it back on my head, Coach Patterson called a time out, and we all ran to the bench.

"She did that on purpose!" Livy shouted, her face bright red and her temper flaring.

"She probably did," Coach Patterson agreed. "Francie, do you want me to say something to her coach?"

"Please don't!" I pleaded quickly, while Livy looked at me like I had lost my mind. "Coach, can you pull me out of the game? I don't want to play anymore today."

"Are you sure, Francie?" Coach asked. "There's no reason for me to pull you out. You did nothing wrong."

"I'm just not feeling well, Coach. Please pull me out," I answered, fighting back tears. Coach Patterson nodded and told Allison to go back into the game.

On the ride home, everyone was quiet, even Suzie. I asked Mom and Dad if I could quit the team. They had a rule about quitting. Once you joined a sport, you had to at least finish out the season, but I was hoping they would make an exception.

"Please don't make me play," I begged from the back seat. "I don't want to play basketball ever again."

"Come on, Francie!" Mom coaxed as she reached back and grabbed my hand. Dad didn't say anything, but I could tell he was clenching his teeth like he does when he's upset. I even saw him wipe his eyes a few times on the long drive home. Neither of them gave me an answer, but later that night, they both came into my room to tuck me into bed.

"Francie, we're so sorry that happened to you today," Dad emphasized, while Mom sat on the bed beside me, rubbing my back. "I hope you know it wasn't your fault, but we'd really like you to reconsider and continue playing basketball. It's time that you can spend with Livy and your other friends. Please don't let that mean girl win and cause you to quit."

"I know it wasn't my fault, but don't you see ... I can't take the chance of losing my hat in front of all of those people, any people, ever again. Please let me quit. I'm not even good. They don't even need me."

"How about if you try something else, Francie?" Mom suggested. "You can quit if you try something else."

"I don't want to try something else! I just want to stay home! Please just let me stay home," I yelled and then I cried big loud sobs into my pillow. My parents stayed in my room, Mom rubbing my back, neither of them saying anything, until I guess I fell asleep.

08
Endless Excuses

The next morning, I woke up with a pounding headache. I must have slept through dinner and straight through the night. I thought about what happened at the game yesterday and rolled into the corner of my bed next to the wall. I didn't want to get up, even though I'd been in bed for more than twelve hours. It was Sunday, and I could hear my family in the kitchen eating breakfast. I thought back to last Sunday at church. Mr. Smith had complimented my outfit, and Mrs. Felix, the elderly lady who sat in front of us, grabbed my arm and told me she liked my earrings and stuck a dollar in my hand as we reached our seats. I know they both meant well, but I could see the sadness in their eyes. They felt sorry for me, the little girl who was losing her hair. It was nice, though; certainly better than that new family, with the four boys who all turned their heads in unison, like a four-headed monster, to look at me, before whispering to their Mom as we walked past them. Mom had grabbed my hand just as I saw Suzie give them the stink eye. She wanted to give them her usual, "She has alopecia" speech, but Dad had put his arm around her and led her to the pew. Today, I wasn't sure if I could deal with the stares and the whispers, or even the pitying compliments. Just then, Mom popped her head into my room.

"Are you coming down for pancakes, Francie?" she asked.

"I'm not feeling the greatest," I moaned. "I think I'm going to stay in bed."

My stomach growled as the smell of pancakes and sausages filled my nostrils, but I knew if I got up for breakfast, I'd be expected to also go to church. Plus, it was easier to fake sickness from your bed. Mom came over and felt my head.

"Well, you don't have a fever, Francie, but okay. Try to get up and move around while we're at church. Maybe you'll feel better." She kissed my forehead and walked to the door. "I'll leave you a plate in the kitchen in case you get hungry after we leave." She winked as she closed the door behind her.

Once the house was quiet, I went downstairs to the kitchen. My plate of pancakes and sausages sat on the counter, wrapped in cellophane. I removed the cellophane and popped my breakfast in the microwave. I ate every delicious bite, tempted to lick my syrupy plate clean. I put my dish in the sink and, instead of going back to bed, I decided to sit on the couch and watch TV until everyone came back from church.

The rest of the day was a flurry of activity all around me, but I just stayed on the couch. Dad sat down with me while Mom took Suzie to a play date and then went to the grocery store. He was folding laundry while we watched Say Yes to the Dress.

"How are you feeling, Bug?" he asked.

"I'm fine, Dad," I lied, faking a cough. "I'm sure it's just a cold." The truth was I was fine because I was home, but I had no desire to go anywhere else, ever again.

"Do you want to go to Suzie's game with us later? She plays at 4:00."

"Nah," I declined. "I think I'll stay here."

I didn't intend to stay home from school the next day, but when I woke up, I had that feeling again. I just didn't want to get out of my bed. I forced a cough when I heard Mom coming upstairs to wake me. It was surprisingly easy to convince her, probably because I was never sick and never missed school. Prior to the 5th grade, I'd always loved going to school. I loved seeing Livy and my other friends every day, and school work had always come pretty easily for me.

When I missed school again on Tuesday, Mom suggested that maybe Livy could bring me my homework.

"Good idea!" I agreed, probably with a little too much enthusiasm for a sick person. I missed Livy, and I was getting kind of bored.

"Come in!" I yelled from the couch when I heard Livy at the front door. She opened the door and came in with some books and worksheets, and some notes from our teachers.

"How are you feeling? she asked. "I've missed you at school."

"I'm okay," I mumbled. "Thanks for bringing me my work."

"When do you think you'll be back?" she asked. "Will you be at practice tomorrow?"

"About that," I replied. "I'm quitting the team. You know ... I just can't deal with all of the stares and the looks, and when that girl knocked off my hat ..." I couldn't finish. I hated even thinking about it.

"I know," Livy empathized. "I totally get it. I used to feel that way about being tall. Everyone would stare at me and make comments. I know this is different, what you're going through, but after a while I started to see there were advantages to being tall, and I tried to focus on them."

"I wish there were advantages to being bald," I admitted. "But I can't think of any."

Livy laughed, "Well, my mom said when you're older you might not have to shave your legs!"

I laughed too as we both looked at my hairless legs and arms.

"I guess that's true," I chuckled. Livy could always find something positive to say.

Mom made spaghetti for dinner and invited Livy to stay. We worked on our homework together, and it felt so great to have her there in my safe space, my home. I thought about the people

I could be myself with (hairless and hatless): Mom, Dad, Suzie, Livy. If I could just stay in my house with them all day every day, life would be good.

By Wednesday afternoon, Mom revealed I was going to have to either go back to school or go see Dr. Schaeffer, our pediatrician. "You know, you need a note if you miss more than three days," she said. "And tomorrow will be your fourth."

"Mom," I started, not knowing how to say this, "I've been thinking. Maybe you should homeschool me, at least until my hair grows back, well ... if it grows back." I put my head in my hands. I couldn't stand to see the look on her face. "I just don't want to go back," I cried. "It's so much easier here. And I'll do the work. You know I can do the work."

Mom sighed and dabbed at her eyes. "Honey," she asserted, "you can't just stay home for the rest of your life. You need to get back to your routine."

"I'm just not ready," I cried. "Please don't make me go back!"

09

DADDY DAUGHTER DAY

On Saturday, Dad announced that we were going on a road trip, just the two of us. "We're going to Harrisburg for a support group meeting. It's a long drive, but I think it'll be worth it for you to meet some other children with alopecia." I don't think he expected me to smile, but I couldn't believe that there were actually other children with alopecia. I thought I was the only one.

The meeting was at a recreation center where they had a basketball court and some obstacle courses and other things. There were about twenty people there, with about five younger kids playing on a jungle gym while their parents stood nearby and talked. Dad and I walked over to some other parents who were sitting at the far end of the room talking.

"My name is Ed," Dad introduced himself, "and this is my daughter, Francie. Francie was diagnosed with alopecia about a month ago."

"My name is John," the tall gentleman greeted, "and this is my wife, Donna. Our daughter, Allie, has had alopecia since she was five. She's over there with the other kids playing basketball."

The other man introduced himself as Pete. "My son, Mark, has had alopecia most of his life. He's over there playing basketball, too." Pete pointed in the direction of the kids at the courts. "Mark's hair comes and goes. Recently, it fell out, and we decided to start coming to the meetings again."

"My name is Mary," stated the other woman in the group. "My daughter, Kate, is playing basketball, too. She's had alopecia since she was about six. She hasn't had any hair since."

I excused myself and walked over to the basketball court. I'd decided to wear my black beanie today, but I was already feeling like I could have left it in the car. Mark introduced himself and the two girls as I got to the court. Mark was completely bald with no eyebrows or eyelashes, and he wore nothing on his head. Allie had patchy hair and one eyebrow. Kate also was completely bald and wore a big, stretchy pink headband around her head. It was still clear she was bald, but it looked pretty.

"Hi, I'm Francie," I offered. "Nice to meet you all."

Mark suggested a game of Horse.

"Sure," I agreed.

He passed me the ball and I took the first shot, but I missed. Kate rebounded the ball and shot a layup. Mark imitated her layup and made it, but Allie missed it.

"H," we all said in unison. I made my layup and, as Kate shot her next basket, I threw my beanie to the side of the court. No one noticed or even looked over as Kate's shot swirled out of the basket. Mark rebounded and banked the ball off the backboard for another basket.

After a few games, we decided to take a break. They each grabbed a water, Kate got some pretzels, and the rest of us found a table away from the parents and other adults.

"So, how long have you had alopecia?" Allie asked me.

I was caught off guard only because I was having so much fun that I had forgotten why Dad and I had driven an hour to be here today.

"About a month," I answered. "How about you?"

"I barely remember having hair," Kate recalled. "I see pictures of myself with hair, and it's hard to believe it's me."

"How have the kids at school been treating you?" Mark asked. "I know they can be tough."

"Well," I remarked, "honestly, it's been super rough." And then, without even thinking about holding back, I told them all about the spit balls and the stares and the whispers. I even told them about the basketball game.

"That's the worst," Mark agreed "I remember when I was in third grade, and these boys on the bus just waited for me every day. They called me 'baldie' and 'ugly' and all kinds of names. I'm not going to tell you it was easy, but my mom always told me to have a comeback. Think of something to give it right back to them. I tried that, and eventually I think they got sick of me not acting like a victim. They eventually started to leave me alone."

"I was excluded from some birthday parties and play dates when I was younger," Kate admitted. "I think my mom was more upset by it than I was. I learned pretty quickly that you're not going to get invited to every party, but all you need is that one good friend that always has your back. My best friend Lexie is great and that helps a lot."

I thought of Livy and knew it could be a lot worse. At least I knew that Livy would always be on my side.

On the drive home, I thanked Dad for taking me to the support group meeting and told him how strangely comfortable it was being with my new friends.

"That's the best thing about support groups," Dad said. "You realize you're not alone and that other people are going through the exact same thing as you."

Exactly, I thought. I wished Mark, Kate, and Allie went to my school, but knowing they were out there, even if they lived far away, helped me somehow.

10

COMEBACK KID

It's not like the support group cured me, not at all, but I knew I couldn't really stay home from school forever, and Mom wasn't buying the homeschool idea. Dad and I continued to go to the meetings every other Saturday. It was a long drive, but we both thought it was worth it. Sometimes Mom came, but it kind of became Dad and my "thing," which was cool.

School was still a drag, but Mark was right. I needed a comeback for Jack and Brandon. I needed to get rid of them once and for all.

"We need a comeback for Jack and Brandon when they throw spit balls in my hair," I told Livy at lunch on Monday. "What do you think we should say?"

"I know what I want to say," she joked. "I still think we should tell Mr. Hartman."

"Let's just try it my way for a few days. I met some kids with alopecia this weekend—"

"What?" Livy interrupted. "Francie! That's great! I didn't even know if there were any other—"

I interrupted her this time. "I know, Liv, me neither!" I smiled. "But let's just see if what they told me works. I want to do this on my own. Try and follow my lead."

About halfway through math class, I thought I was in the clear when Mr. Hartman turned to write something on the board, and I felt something hit the back of my head. At least I didn't have any hair left, so the spit ball just bounced off my hat and landed on my desk. By the end of class, there was a small pile of spit balls on my desk and more on the floor. I stood up, turned around, and tried not to sound nervous as I loudly demanded, "Are you guys going to clean these up?"

The whole class was watching as I packed my backpack and headed toward the door with Livy right behind me. As we were leaving the classroom, I looked back and saw Mr. Hartman walking toward Jack and Brandon. "Yeah, that's probably a good idea, guys," he agreed, handing them a dustpan and brush.

The next day, Mr. Hartman announced that we were going to switch seats.
"Brandon and Jack, I think you'll be less distracted in the front row," he decided. Livy and I moved to our new seats a few rows behind them. I hadn't wanted to be a tattletale, but I was happy I had listened to Mark's advice and stood up for myself. Plus, I was happy Mr. Hartman was paying attention. In addition to having a best friend like Livy, it was always helpful to have adults who have my back, too. With the boys in front of us as we walked out of class, Livy fist-bumped me. We were making progress!

11

Drawing on the Benefits of Art

"I think I want to take a drawing class," I told Mom on Saturday.
"That's wonderful, honey!" she said. "Let's see what they have at the Art Institute. I think that's a great idea!"

We went to the store to buy some new pencils and a sketch book for my new class. Mom also bought me a bright pink messenger bag to keep all of my art supplies in one place. I was super nervous to meet new people, but very excited to draw and learn new ways to make my drawings better.

"Maybe I should talk to your teacher or the class and tell them about your alopecia," Mom suggested on the way to class.

"It's okay, Mom," I assured her, thinking I could handle it. But, as we pulled up, I changed my mind and asked her to walk in with me. I hadn't really thought about the fact that no one here knew me or why I was going bald. At least at school, Mom had told the teachers and some parents, so I never really had to explain myself.

Mom and I walked into the Art Institute. We were a few minutes early, so we went straight to the classroom, hoping the art teacher would be there. We peaked inside, and there she was, a pretty lady with short brown hair, wearing jeans and a t-shirt with a smock over top.

"Hi, I'm Mrs. Winston," she greeted, extending her hand to me.

"Hi, I'm Francie!" I introduced myself as I shook her hand.

Mom introduced herself, too, and reached out her hand. "Francie and I decided to come in a little early so we could tell you about her alopecia," she explained.

"Alopecia?" asked Mrs. Winston. "My aunt has alopecia. I'm very familiar with it."

"You're kidding!" Mom exclaimed. She winked at me then looked back at Mrs. Winston, "Then I guess I don't have to explain to you why Francie is wearing a hat."

"Hats are fine in here," Mrs. Winston replied, "and no hats are fine as well." She looked at me when she added, "My aunt actually wears a wig. She doesn't talk about her alopecia at all, not even to her family and close friends. It is very brave of you, Francie, to embrace your alopecia and tell people about it. My aunt is a very sad woman. She doesn't go out much, and she spends a lot of time fixing her wig and perfecting her make up to hide her alopecia from the world. I'm sure it's not easy, and I admire your courage.

"Now, let's get you set up to draw," she suggested, just as a few other students came around the corner.

"Hi, I'm Mrs. Winston," she offered to the kids walking in. Mom tapped my shoulder and slipped out while Mrs. Winston introduced herself to the other students.

Mrs. Winston directed us to a big square table where we each took a seat.

"Let's go around the room and introduce ourselves," she suggested. "Francie, why don't you start?"

"Hi, I'm Francie," I said quietly.

"Hi, I'm Mallory," added a girl I recognized from school.

"Hi, I'm Tommy," greeted a boy with freckles and glasses.

There were eight students in our class all together. I only recognized two from school, Mallory and another boy, Michael. The other kids in the class went to public school or were homeschooled.

"Let's get started," Mrs. Winston advised, and she introduced our first technique: feathering.

We were all pretty quiet during the first class. Two of the girls, Sammy and Natasha, seemed to know each other, so they chatted while they drew, and the rest of us just focused on our work.

12
Putting on Courage

The following Saturday at drawing class, I kept to myself again, much like I did at school. While drawing, though, I started to realize that I didn't care or pay attention to whether or not people were looking at me. I only cared about what was in front of me and making it perfect. I drew trees and animals and was even starting to draw faces. Maybe it was because I didn't care, but the other kids in the class didn't seem to notice or talk about my alopecia, either. There was no whispering like at school. Sammy and Natasha continued to chat throughout class, and some of the other students would join in while drawing, talking about their day or friends at school, but I just listened and focused on my artwork.

After class, Mrs. Winston asked to talk to me.

"You're a talented artist, Francie," she praised. "But that's not what I want to talk to you about. I was wondering if you wanted to tell the other students about your alopecia. A few of them have asked me about it, but not in a mean way. They're generally concerned about you and your health. Maybe it would help if you told them about your alopecia?"

I'd never thought about that, but I definitely needed some time to think.

"It's your choice, Francie," Mrs. Winston assured me. "I'll support you whatever you decide."

"It can't hurt," Dad said when I told my parents about Mrs. Winston's suggestion over dinner. "At the very least, it'll let everyone know that you aren't sick and don't have cancer."

"I don't know," I sighed. "What if they laugh?"

"Why would they laugh, honey?" Mom asked.

"Hmm," Dad hummed thoughtfully. "It's going to take some courage to talk in front of all those kids, right?"

"Right," I replied, wondering where he was going with this.

"Just like it takes courage to take off your hat in front of strangers, right?"

"Right," I repeated, this time getting a little nervous.

"I have an idea," Dad offered. Even Mom looked uncomfortable. Dad suggested we drive to the mall; not the local one, but the bigger one that was about forty-five minutes away. Once inside, he stated, "Okay, Francie, you don't see anyone you know here, right?"

"No," I said, biting my lower lip. "I don't think so."

"Okay then. You and I are going to walk down to the pretzel shop. Here, give me your hat," He requested, trying to be all no-big-deal. I knew there was a catch.

"Dad! What?" I put both hands on my head.

"Come on, Bug! You can do this. Just put on your courage!"

I only did it because I figured we wouldn't know anyone, but I handed Dad my hat. We walked to the pretzel shop, and he passed my hat back to me.

"You did it, Bug!" He pulled me into a hug. "I knew you could do it!" We walked back and forth a few times. Each time I took off my hat, a few people stared at me. One elderly lady didn't take her eyes off me as I passed her seat. After, when I should have been long out of her view, I could still feel her eyes on me.

"Just smile at them, Bug. They're not being mean. They're just uneducated. Maybe someday you'll feel comfortable enough to teach people about alopecia, but for now, come on. Let's walk one more time."

We walked back towards the shoe store where we started and, as we passed that same lady, I smiled at her and she instinctively smiled back.

"Good job, Bug!" Dad praised when we got into the car. "You're braver than you think, you know."

The next day I talked to Livy about what Dad and I had done. "Your dad!" She laughed, throwing her head back. "He's nuts, but I think he's right. And I think you need to talk to your drawing class. Maybe it would have been better here at school if you had talked to the school."

"The whole school! Are you crazy, Livy?"

You know what I mean," she clarified. "And, besides, it's only seven kids. You can do this, Francie. You're braver than you think."

The next week, I told Mrs. Winston that I would do it: I'd actually talk to the class and tell them about my alopecia. Mrs. Winston asked me if I wanted to stand to talk to them or if I would be more comfortable talking to them from my seat. I decided that I would remain seated. That way, if it became necessary, I could just slide under the table and stay there until the end of class.

"Good morning, everyone," Mrs. Winston announced. "Today, before we get started, Francie wants to talk to you about something."

Suddenly, fourteen eyes were on me, sixteen counting Mrs. Winston. I thought maybe now would be a good time to slide under the table, but, instead, I remembered what Dad said. I put on my courage like a suit of armor, and I just opened my mouth and hoped that the words would come out.

"Hi. As you know, I'm Francie," I started. My voice was so shaky, but I continued. "You might be wondering why I wear a hat every day to class, and why I only have one eyebrow and no eyelashes." Some of the kids nodded their heads, but they all looked at me intently. Mrs. Winston smiled and winked.

"Well, I have a disease called alopecia. Basically, my body is allergic to my hair, so it falls out. I'm not sick. Besides not having much hair, I'm a regular kid. Just like you, I like to draw. I also love to play basketball and hang out with my friends and my family. I just started going bald about two months ago."

"Does anyone have any questions?" Mrs. Winston asked.

"Does it hurt when your hair falls out?" Michael, who sat next to me, asked.

"Nope, not at all," I answered.

"Is it contagious?" inquired Sam, who sat across from me.

"Nope, you can't catch it," I replied.

"You don't need to wear a hat, you know," mentioned Mallory, who sat next to Paige.

I looked at Mallory and thought about what Gertie had said. Did Mallory really mean it?

"That's very nice of you, Mallory," Mrs. Winston said. "Maybe someday Francie will feel comfortable enough to take off her hat. Right, Francie?"

I smiled at Mrs. Winston. I was glad I'd decided to talk to the class, but I wasn't sure about taking my hat off just yet.

13
A Moment of Bravery, Enduring Courage

Each week at drawing class, the other students and I talked more as we drew. When we got to class, Mrs. Winston would describe the new technique we were trying that day and then we'd all focus on our work while chatting about other things. I enjoyed my time at art class so much and looked forward to it all week. We all came to drawing class because we loved to draw and wanted to get better at it. It was nice to have that common bond, kind of like the common bond of alopecia that I shared with Mark and Allie and Kate. I felt closer to these students in drawing class than I did to most of my classmates--except Livy, of course--and I noticed that when I saw Mallory and Michael in school, they'd now smile and say hello. I also recognized that the stares and the whispering were not as bad as they once were.
I shared with Mrs. Baldwin, my art teacher at school, some of the techniques I'd learned at the institute. I was proud and confident when I talked about drawing techniques, because I knew what I was talking about now. It was something I was good at, like Livy in basketball.

"I'd like to let you co-teach our next lesson with me," Mrs. Baldwin told me one morning, "We're going to learn about shading, and you've mastered that skill. I'd love your help, if you don't mind." I was a little nervous to stand in front of the class, but I loved to talk about drawing, and shading had become my favorite technique. I clipped my drawing to the board like Mrs. Baldwin sometimes did and addressed my class.
"I use shading in two different ways," I explained. "The first way is with all of the lines going the same way, and the second is in patches." I showed them how to shade using both techniques. The students in the class were very interested and asked me questions about shading. I showed them examples, and even

came over to their desks to demonstrate for them.

"How do I get the house in my drawing to stand out?" Jenna asked.

"I'd use shading with all of your lines going in the same direction for that," I explained.

"How do I add texture?" Eric asked. I walked over to his desk and held up his drawing.

"See," I told the class. "Eric's drawing would be a good example of using patches." I showed Eric how to draw lines going in all different directions to help add definition to the face he'd drawn. I was walking back to the board from Eric's desk when Jack raised his hand in the back.

"Yes, Jack?" I paused.

"Why do you wear a hat to school?" he asked.

I could feel my face turn bright red as my classmates and Mrs. Baldwin gasped.

"Jack! Go to the principal's office," Mrs. Baldwin pointed at the door.

Wait!" I yelled, louder than I intended, "Mrs. Baldwin, let me answer his question."

Jack sat back down, tentatively.

"I wear a hat because I have alopecia," I answered. "It's an autoimmune disease, but I'm not sick. My hair just fell out."

A few people laughed nervously, but mostly they listened and, just like at the institute, they asked many of the same questions.

"Is it contagious?"

"Does it hurt?"

"Will it grow back?"

One at a time, I answered each and every question as best as I could.

"I don't know if it'll grow back," I responded to the last question, "but I'm a regular kid like you. I'm just bald."

Mallory, from the Art Institute, raised her hand.

"You don't need to wear a hat, you know," she declared.

"Yeah, why do you wear a hat?" Jack repeated his original question.

I looked at Mallory and smiled. Then I looked at Livy in the back row. She winked at me, and I smiled back. I thought about Mrs. Winston and her aunt's sadness. I wondered what Gertie would think, but I also thought about Mark and Kate and Allie and their courage.

"You know what?" I replied. "You're right!" And in a moment of bravery, I whipped off my hat and threw it to Livy in the back of the classroom, revealing my bald head.

Livy picked up the hat from the ground and carried it back up to me, hugging me as she said,

"I'm so proud of you. Now, can you come back to the basketball team?"

I hugged Livy back and looked over my shoulder at Mallory who gave me a thumbs-up.

"See you on Saturday," I mouthed, excited to see what Mrs. Winston and everyone else would say when I took off my hat at drawing class.

Walking out of class with my friends, I couldn't help but feel proud of what I'd accomplished. It now seemed a little silly how nervous I had been to stand in front of my class and teach them art techniques. But finding the courage to do so made me feel brave and strong enough to share my alopecia story. I could get used to this courage thing!

AUTHOR BIO

After dreaming of being a writer all of her life, Betsy engaged in some freelance writing and editing. She and her husband Jeff have four daughters: Helena, Maddie, Sofie, and Mimi. The most significant and unexpected part of Betsy's story occurred when Maddie lost all of her hair at age 5. Soon after, Betsy and Jeff founded the Children's Alopecia Project (CAP), now an international organization that focuses on building self-esteem in children with alopecia. Helping grateful children and parents has blessed Betsy and her family in ways they would never have known had they not first been "gifted" with a very challenging time and diagnosis for their family. Francie's story of courage is loosely based on Maddie's own journey of living with alopecia. For more information on CAP, visit childrensalopeciaproject.org.

This book is dedicated to Maddie, whose quiet confidence and unwavering courage have inspired me and left me in awe since October 2003.

FROM MADDIE

I'd like to thank my parents, first and foremost, for allowing me to take my alopecia journey at my own pace. Doing so has had the biggest impact in my life. My parents always allowed me to express myself in any way that I felt comfortable. They did not force me to wear a hat or wig to cover up in public. They gave me total freedom to be whoever I wanted to be, and that has helped me become the person I am today, beyond just alopecia. They taught me not to compare my journey to anyone else's and to commend myself for my progress, even just the small victories. And most importantly, my parents taught me not to beat myself up for falling off track sometimes or for not being where I wanted to be at that exact moment because I would get there someday. And I have.

So thank you Mom and Dad, for letting me take the lead and also for starting the Children's Alopecia Project. Without you and CAP, I would not be where I am today, and I am forever grateful for your love and support.

I would also like to thank Devon (AKA Francie's best friend, Livy), who means more to me than she probably will ever realize. To her, I was just her best friend who had similar interests and hobbies, but to me, she was the first person outside of my family who saw me for ME, and I cannot thank her enough for that. She made me forget that I even had alopecia which, at the time, was so important to me. She not only was a distraction that made me feel better when I was first going through losing my hair, but she showed me what true friendship meant. Outside of my family, she was the one thing that was consistent in my life when everything else seemed to be changing. I am so grateful to have had a friend like her back then, and even more grateful now to still have this person in my life. Thank you, Devon. If it wasn't for you, I would probably still be the sad, shy girl who didn't talk to anyone because she was scared of kids judging her and not liking her for the way she was. I am so proud to be your best friend.

Love,
Maddie

Made in the USA
Columbia, SC
09 August 2020